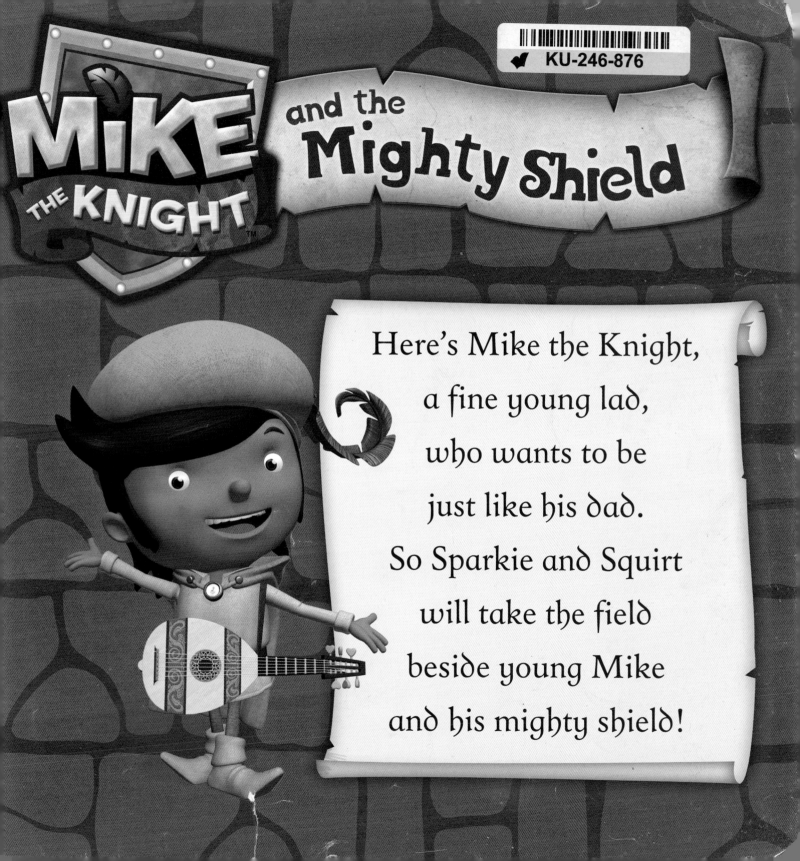

Mike THE KNIGHT

and the Mighty Shield

Here's Mike the Knight,
a fine young lad,
who wants to be
just like his dad.
So Sparkie and Squirt
will take the field
beside young Mike
and his mighty shield!

Great knights are always prepared –
you never know when you'll run
into a rowdy Viking!

Mike spotted a painting of his dad.
"Whoa! Look at Dad bouncing
Vikings off his shield!"

"That's how knights test their shields," explained the Queen. "Vikings love bouncing almost as much as they love jam tarts!"

This gave Mike an idea – "I'll try bouncing with my shield! Not with real Vikings, of course. But I know two dragons who will help."

As the three friends ran down the tower steps, Mike spotted the shield from the painting.

"Hmmm," said Mike. "What if my shield isn't the best? I know! I'll bounce with this one instead."

Sparkie lifted the mighty shield down. "Are you sure, Mike? It's very heavy."

"Yes, all I need is a little practice. **By the King's crown, that's it!** I'm Mike the Knight and my mission is to bounce Vikings with the greatest shield in all of Glendragon!"

Mike raced to his bedroom and pulled the secret lever to put on his armour. Now ready for action, Mike drew his enchanted sword. "A jam tart?"

Mike ignored the jam tart. "Now that I've got a new shield, you can have my old one, Squirt."

"But look, Mike!" Squirt said. "Your old shield has a button – wow! It makes it bigger!"

"My new, mighty shield has lots of buttons. It is the biggest and the best!" declared Mike.

Mike could barely lift his new, heavy shield. "Could you carry this for me Sparkie? I'm...err...saving my strength for bouncing."

When they reached the beach, Sparkie handed the mighty shield to Mike, who wobbled under its weight.

"Just getting my balance," Mike mumbled. "Right, Sparkie, you run at me and I'll bounce you off my shield."

Sparkie, wearing his special Viking hat, started to run towards Mike, but Mike couldn't see over the mighty shield and fell over!

"Are you sure you don't want to use your old shield?" asked Sparkie.

Meanwhile, out at sea, a group of Vikings heard funny noises coming from the shore.

"You need to be more like a Viking, Sparkie. That's the problem," said Mike, as he propped the shield up. "Vikings are noisy, and they crash into things and do somersaults!"

Sparkie stomped along the beach and did a forward roll while he shouted "Øøørg! Snørg! Høørgh!"

But the Vikings heard Sparkie's noises and rowed even faster towards them.

Squirt was on the other side of the beach, practising how best to hold his lovely new shield. He could even throw it in the air and catch it!

Squirt was bouncing imaginary Vikings off his shield when
the real Vikings jumped off their boat and tried to grab
Squirt's shield.

"Hee-eee-lllllppp!" he cried while he tried to keep
the shield away from the Vikings.

"Oh, no!" cried Mike. He thought for a moment. "Mum said Vikings love jam tarts even more than bouncing."

Mike quickly pulled out his enchanted sword to reveal the huge jam tart. He waved it above his head and shouted towards the Vikings, "Jam tart! Jam tart!"

The Vikings spun around – "Jøøm tøørt! Jøøm tøørt!"

Mike flung the jam tart as far away from Squirt as possible and the Vikings sprinted after it.

"I'm sorry, Squirt…may I have my old shield back?
Dad's shield is too heavy for me," Mike finally admitted.

"Yes! Take it! I can't keep it away from the Vikings
anymore!" Squirt said happily. "Errr…do you have any
more tarts, Mike?"

"No, but I have my shield.
**It's time to be a knight
and do it right!"**
Mike shouted.

He was ready to bounce
some Vikings!

The Vikings were so excited when they saw the shield – "Shøøøld! Bøøørgh!" They started bouncing on the ground.

"Do you think your little shield will bounce them?" asked Sparkie worriedly.

"I have to try!" Mike said.

Mike pushed the button on his shield to make it bigger. "Come on, shield! Please bounce for me!"

The first Viking ran at Mike's shield and bounced perfectly, as did the other two!

Mike angled his shield and bounced each Viking straight back into their boat. Sparkie quickly pushed the boat off the beach. At last all the Vikings were gone!

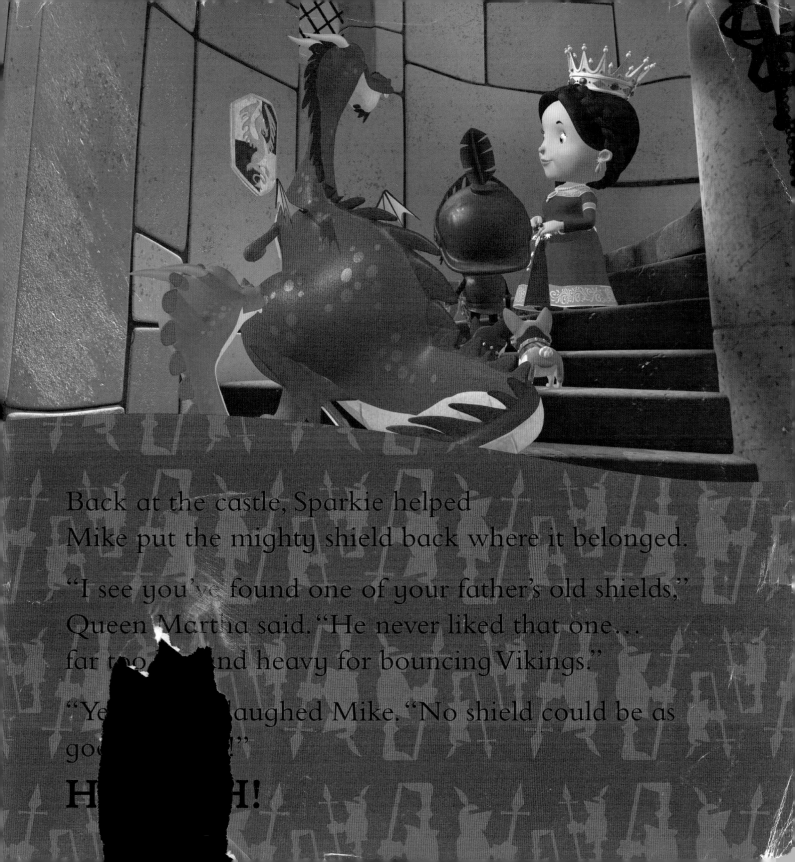

Back at the castle, Sparkie helped
Mike put the mighty shield back where it belonged.

"I see you've found one of your father's old shields,"
Queen Martha said. "He never liked that one...
far too ▓▓▓ and heavy for bouncing Vikings."

"Ye▓▓▓ ▓▓ ▓aughed Mike. "No shield could be as
goo▓ ▓▓ ▓▓!"

H▓▓▓H!

More magical Mike the Knight books coming soon... HUZZAH!

For Steven, Matthew & Jonathan
- M.F.

For Lupin
- P.L.

For Ben O'Donnell
- B.O'D.

Text copyright © 2009 Mel Fisher
Illustrations copyright © 2009 Patricia Ludlow

First published in Ireland by O'Donnell Press 2009
12 Coolemoyne Park, Jordanstown, Co. Antrim BT37 0RP
Telephone: 028 9096 6493
Email: b.odonnell93@ntlworld.com
www.odonnellpress.com

Special thanks to Paul Porter.

A CIP catalogue record of this book is available from the British Library.

Printed in Ireland by GPS Colour Graphics Ltd.

ISBN 978-0-9553325-7-9

1 2 3 4 5 6 7 8 9 10

O'DONNELL PRESS

The Dolphin of Dingle Bay

By Mel Fisher

Illustrated by Patricia Ludlow

The gravel crunched as the car wheels ground to a halt and the door was flung open. A young boy leapt out and began to run. Across the path, over the stile and through the fields he ran, as fast as he could. He kept running until he could taste the salt from the sea air. He kept running until the wind caught his cap and lifted it high above him.

Sean jumped to catch his cap but the sea breeze lifted it higher. He chased his cap all the way to the lighthouse, jumping and laughing as it dipped and swirled in the wind.

At the door of the lighthouse stood an old man, stooped with age, smoking a pipe. His wrinkled face gazed out into the bay. He didn't even turn his head when Sean came alongside him.

"Is he there?" asked Sean.
"No, haven't seen him for days," replied the old man.
"But he'll be back. He always comes back."

Patiently they waited, watching in vain for Fungi the Dingle
Bay dolphin. In the distance Sean heard a call for supper;
he sighed and slowly climbed the path back up to the cottage.

Early the next morning Sean rushed to the lighthouse. The look on the lighthouse keeper's face told him Fungi was back.

Sean smiled as he climbed down onto the rocks, waving and whistling as Fungi jumped and dived over the surf.

Soon Sean's Dad arrived in a boat and the soft purr of the engine made Fungi leap out of the water. He flipped backwards and plunged into the water right beside them. There were squeals of laughter from Sean and his Dad as the sea water showered over them.

"Ok Sean, it's time to go. I see Fungi is ready." Sean's Dad grinned as he tossed his son a life jacket. "Let's hope the fish are biting today."

The early morning mist began to lift and the sea glistened as it caught the sunlight. They stopped just off the Blasket Islands and Sean's Dad baited for sea bass while Sean fished with his old fishing net. Fungi often helped by giving Sean a freshly caught fish.

Sean would throw it into the bucket as his dad pulled a face. "Oh, to be a dolphin," sighed his father, as he reeled in another empty line.

Fungi was in a strange mood that day and he kept racing out towards the ocean and then turning to click and squeak.
"Dad, I think he wants us to follow him."
"Well, there are no fish here today, so maybe he knows where to find some."
They followed Fungi into rougher seas, watching him as he broke through the swelling waves with ease.

Now they could see why Fungi was leading them out of the bay, for just ahead loomed a large pod of dolphins. As these graceful, gentle creatures dived in and out of the water, Fungi clicked with excitement. This was obviously where he had been when Sean had arrived in Dingle.

Suddenly Fungi disappeared under the waves and Sean moved to the bow of the boat to check where he had gone. As he climbed over the tackle box a large wave rocked the boat and Sean fell forward hitting his head. Losing his balance, he tumbled overboard into the sea. He felt as if he was falling through the water forever.

Suddenly Fungi was there beside him, reassuring Sean with his deep friendly eyes. Fungi offered him a flipper and flicked his tail and the two of them swam swiftly through the water.

Sean swam alongside rays, while watching giant jellyfish billow their skirts and spider crabs scurry across rocks. He dived in the shadow of an enormous leatherback turtle, and lost count of the jewel anemones smothering the rocks.

Sean was enjoying every minute of his adventure, twirling
and twisting with Fungi. As they raced through the water
Sean reached out to catch a piece of seaweed caught up in the
currents. Suddenly out of nowhere another dolphin appeared
and stole it from his hand. Sean laughed and tried to catch
the seaweed. But the dolphin was too quick and flicked the
seaweed up into the water above them. Then like lightning
Fungi moved in letting Sean reclaim the seaweed and they
raced off, with the other dolphin in friendly pursuit.

Amidst all the fuss Sean heard his father call his name and Fungi followed the voice to surface just beside their boat. With the biggest smile ever Sean gave his dad the thumbs up and reached for a hand into the boat.

"Wow!" he said, "I sure would love to do that again."

"I don't think so!" came a reply from his father.
Sean opened his eyes, blinking with the strong sunlight.
He could just make out his dad's face peering down at him.
"You gave me quite a shock with that fall out of the boat,"
his dad explained.
"Where are we?" mumbled Sean.
"Back at the lighthouse. You've been muttering about
dolphins the whole way across the bay," teased his dad.

"But Dad I've had such fun.... I've seen spider crabs....
and leatherback turtles.... and been chased by dolphins...."
stuttered Sean.
"Shhh now, you've been dreaming. You knocked yourself
out as you fell into the water," said his Dad.

Sean sat up slowly with a puzzled look, for in his hand was a
tattered piece of wet seaweed. Surely it hadn't been just a
dream? He looked up at the old lighthouse keeper, his eyes
searching the old man's weather-beaten face for an answer.
But the old man only smiled and said, "That's just the magic
of Dingle Bay, my boy." But his eyes sparkled with mischief
as he reached into the bucket and threw Fungi a fish.

Enjoy more great picture books from
O'Donnell Press

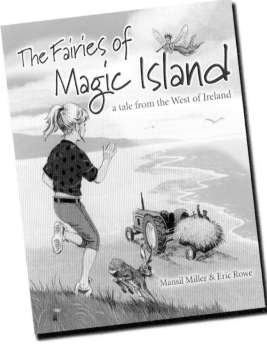

Visit: www.odonnellpress.com